LIVING PAINTING

Sweet Passion

To dear Helena with affection from:
The author,
Jaqueline Polck
30/10/2023

JAQUELINE POLCK

Balboa Press books may be ordered through booksellers or by contacting:

Balboa Press
A Division of Hay House
1663 Liberty Drive
Bloomington, IN 47403
www.balboapress.co.uk
UK TFN: 0800 0148647 (Toll Free inside the UK)
UK Local: 02036 956325 (+44 20 3695 6325 from outside the UK)

ISBN: 978-1-9822-8749-8 (sc)
ISBN: 978-1-9822-8750-4 (e)

Print information available on the last page.

Balboa Press rev. date: 10/16/2023

BALBOA PRESS
A DIVISION OF HAY HOUSE

CHAPTER 1

THE PAINTING

The English countryside, nineteenth century

Albertina walks firmly towards the market in the small town of Brentshe, holding some coins in her right hand, her arms crossed. Her face is serious and sad, hiding little of this young woman's beauty. She seems to be going through a moment of affliction. Walking past the shops, the young woman stops at Mr Will's stall and gazes at the bread.

ALBERTINA: Hello, Mr Will. I'll have one of these. How much are they?

MR WILL: Hello, dear Albertina. I will pack it for you. Here you go. You don't have to pay, my dear. A little help won't hurt.

Albertina looks grateful and smiles at Mr Will. A voice calls for Albertina.

LOLA: Albertina! Albertina!

Lola waves at Albertina.

ALBERTINA: Thank you, Mr Will!

LOLA: Come here, darling. Look, I've saved some milk for you. Come fetch some more later.

ALBERTINA: You're an angel. Thank you for help, Mrs Lola. I hope I can pay you back soon. Thank you. I have to go!

Lola watches Albertina leaving.

LOLA: Poor girl. So young—a widow with a child to raise. Fortunately, she has Mrs Adele to shelter her.

Adele is a lonely lady in her sixties with a slightly thick body and grey hair. She is of Lebanese descent and does not have very delicate features. But she possesses a generous heart.

Albertina walks back home and sees a job advertisement that reads, "Wanted: a beautiful young lady to be portrayed naked in works of art. Signed: Constantino the painter." Albertina knows she is exactly right for this job, and she really needs the money. She takes the paper and goes home. She looks at the paper and smiles, and her heart fills with hope. All she has ever wanted is to be happy and to be able to live with her son, William, a beautiful little boy of three years old. She does not want to depend on others for help or live in Mrs Adele's house. Adele is also poor and rents a small room with a door directly onto the street and Albertina sleeps on a mattress on the floor with her son. Albertina is almost home.

ADELE: William! Do you want to sleep a little more?

William is tired. He looks to Adele.

WILLIAM: No! I'll wait for my mother. She went to buy some food.

William looks down to the opening door and smiles. Albertina comes in. He runs to hug her.

ALBERTINA: How I missed my boy! Look what I've brought!

WILLIAM: I'm starving!

ALBERTINA: Well, let's eat then. Hello, Mrs Adele. How are you?

ADELE: Hello, dear. I am not very well. It's my sister; she is very ill.

Albertina looks scared while she sets the table, seats William on the chair, and pulls the other chair to Mrs Adele.

ALBERTINA: I am sorry. Let's hope she will get better soon. I'll pray for her. If there's anything I can do, please tell me.

ADELE: Yes, let's hope! I am going to her house today. I'll be back tomorrow. How about you? What's this?

ALBERTINA: Ah! I saw this job advertisement. Look! It is to pose for a painter. I am going there shortly. I'll make good money, don't you think?

ADELE: Well! That's great! Yes, it seems to be a good opportunity. I am happy for you. You are young and pretty. You need to find a man to marry!

ALBERTINA: I don't know. It's not that easy to find someone like that. Yes, I am young, but not by much. I'm a widow and have a son. I don't think I have too much hope for my life! Look at me, Mrs Adele. I have no one. I live by charity.

ADELE: I understand you, but I am sure things are going to change. You know, dear, sometimes it takes some time until we have our lives back. When we are young, we want everything very fast.

ALBERTINA: Wise words, but I don't know. I don't want to raise my expectations!

Albertina looks down, full of sadness. A tear rolls down her face. William puts his hands on her shoulders and speaks in a whisper.

WILLIAM: Mummy, I will take care of you!

Adele looks at William with compassionate eyes.

ADELE: All done, gentleman! Well, you are going to make me emotional. I don't want to cry.

ALBERTINA: Thank you, son! You are just like your father. I can't believe he's gone so early. I miss him very much.

William: Will I meet him one day, Mummy?

Albertina takes a deep breath.

Albertina: I don't know, son. Perhaps. Mrs Adele, what time are you leaving for your sister's? I'd like to go to the painter's house to ask about the job.

Adele: Go there, darling. I'll wait for you here with William. I've still got some time.

Albertina thanks her and goes to Constantino's house.

Constantino is sleeping on his sofa when someone knocks on his door. *Knock, knock, knock.* On the other side of the door, Albertina is insistent. *Knock, knock, knock.* Constantino wakes up, scared, and opens the door.

Albertina: Hello! I've come regarding the advertisement … for a girl to pose for Constantino?

Constantino: Yes, come in. What's your name?

Albertina: Albertina! And you? Are you Constantino?

Constantino: Yes, I am. I need a girl to pose nude so I can paint my works. Are you really willing to do that? I need to see your body now. Can you take off your clothes near the window? Don't worry; let's see if this works.

Albertina: Yes, I am willing to do it. To tell the truth, I really need the money!

Constantino: Money? Do you think it's easy to sell a painting? No one here spoke about money. I can only pay if I sell the painting.

Albertina: It's all right. I imagine it isn't easy to sell paintings, but I will take the job because I need it. Shall I take my clothes off then?

Constantino: Yes!

Albertina takes off her dress and gets completely naked. She is a bit embarrassed but stands near the window. Constantino is amazed by her body. Albertina is a charming lady of countryside beauty and the daughter of villagers. Her long brown hair and her blackberry eyes stand out against her silky white skin. With her perfect and delicate features, she looks like a doll.

Albertina has the calm demeanour of an obedient woman. After her parents died in her adolescence, she went to live with her aunt and uncle and her cousin, Felicio, who was four years older. Her aunt was her mother's sister. Albertina, in constant acquaintance with Felicio, who was, by the way, a handsome and presentable lad, ended up falling in love with her cousin and married him. Felicio was a train driver and had a good job, but as fate would have it, the poor girl was widowed after losing her love in a horrible work accident. Felicio's father had already abandoned the house many years ago, and his mother had died of grief in the following years. Having lost her aunt and uncle, Albertina had no one. She was lonely and had nowhere to live. At that time there were no contracts for renting a house. Everything was only agreed upon between the parties. If a person did not have the rent money, they had to leave immediately. But luckily Mrs Adele, Felicio's childhood nanny, had helped Albertina, giving shelter to the beautiful, young woman.

Constantino: You have a beautiful body. Turn sideways and put your hand on the window. Lift your right leg a bit and tilt your body closer to the window. Wow! You are very feminine and pretty with your long hair falling on your hips. Firm and full bosoms! They look perfect for my work. Shall we begin?

Albertina: I can't now. I have to return home.

Constantino: It's all right! It's getting dark and I need light. It will be better tomorrow. What about tomorrow at noon?

Albertina puts on her clothes.

Albertina: Yes, perfect! How long will it take? I have to take care of my son, William. He is only 3 years old.

Constantino: Well, it's a time-consuming job. We need to be patient. It won't be easy; you will need to stand still for a long time. But your child can come along, if you want!

ALBERTINA: So then we will have to be patient with each other. I don't want to bring William here. I don't want him to see it! But I can come as many times as you want.

Constantino looks at her doubtfully, lifts his hand to his hair, and nods.

CONSTANTINO: It's all right then! What about your husband? Where is he?

ALBERTINA: He died six months ago.

CONSTANTINO: That's sad, but you are young and pretty. You'll soon find someone. How old are you?

ALBERTINA: I am twenty-seven. Thank you for your kind words, but I am not considering this now. I still care about my husband.

CONSTANTINO: I see. But he's dead. Whom do you live with?

ALBERTINA: I live at Mrs Adele's. She knew my husband and offered me help.

CONSTANTINO: It is good you have her to help you.

ALBERTINA: Yes, she is like an angel! A strong woman who has been through much sadness in this life. Well, I have to go.

CONSTANTINO: Yes! I'll see you tomorrow.

As Albertina quickly walks back home, she passes through the train station and hears an unusual noise. She stops, listening, and hears the muffled voice of a woman shouting for help. She follows the voice through the pillars inside the train station and found a young woman who was almost raped. Albertina moves fast and hits the man's head with a stone and grabs the girl. They run as fast as they can.

ALBERTINA: Run! Run! Quick! Here, let's hide in this alley.

They find a corner and hide in the free space between houses in a dead-end alley, and with their hearts beating fast, they make a silent gesture to each other. After some time, Albertina peeks her head outside the free space and looks at the main street, observing the movement.

ALBERTINA: Calm down, it's over. He won't come after us. What's your name?

ANNE: I'm Anne! And you?

ALBERTINA: My name is Albertina! My goodness, you are very pale, Anne. Let's go to that shop and ask for help. Come!

The two women enter Mr Phil's shop, a luxurious decor and fabric store. They look at the shelves full of fabrics, seasonal hats, plumes and feathers … all very sophisticated. Mr Phil himself stands right behind the wooden counter: He is wearing a hat and idly chewing on a toothpick, he was thinking far away.

ALBERTINA: Hello, sir. Can you help us?

Mr Phil looks scared and quickly comes out from behind the counter.

ALBERTINA: Hello, sir. Can you help us? She is not feeling well. She is terrified. She was almost raped by a man, but I grabbed her and we ran away!

PHIL: Yes, of course! I'll close the shop and get some water … Here we go! Nice to meet you. I am Phil. Tell me, how is the bastard? I will kill this bloody bastard …

ANNE: Nice to meet you. I'm Anne! Albertina got there just in time, thankfully! Don't you worry, Mr Phil, I am calming down. I am fine. I'll just wait a little longer!

PHIL: Yes, darling, wait here and I'll walk you home.

ALBERTINA: Well, I better go now! Anne, you are in good hands. Now I can calm down. thank you, Mr Phil.

Anne hug Albertina.

ANNE: Thank you for everything. God bless you! You are very brave. I'll never forget you.

Albertina smiles and starts walking away. A few minutes later Mr. Phil is interested in finding out more about Anne.

PHIL: I am sorry for asking, ma'am, but how old are you? Are you married?

ANNE: No problem, Mr Phil. *(laughs)* I am thirty-five. I was engaged for ten years, but he had another family. I've been deceived all this time.

PHIL: My good lord! What a bastard. But you have children?

ANNE: No! I lost two children by him. But God knows what to do. What about you, Mr Phil? How old are you? Are you married?

Phil looks embarrassed and sad, and doesn't want to talk about his life.

PHIL: My life is not interesting, my dear. I am old … forty-eight. Shall we go? It's late. I'll walk you home.

ANNE: Yes, please. I am really tired too. Thank you for everything, Mr Phil. It isn't very far from here!

The two of them walk along the downtown street, arm in arm. Anne watches Mr Phil, he's an elegant man who wears a hat and carries a walking stick.

PHIL: Do you work?

ANNE: No, I don't. But I'd love to!

PHIL: Very well, what are your dreams?

ANNE: I don't have dreams! I have tried to plan my life in the past, and it doesn't work.

PHIL: Oh! I see we are quite alike. I, too, prefer not to dream or expect too much from others.

ANNE: Yes, it's true! Well, I live here …

They gaze at each other without words. Both become shy. Mr Phil looks at the house curiously.

PHIL: So, this is where you live!

ANNE: Mr Phil, I won't invite you in because my mother is not a very pleasant or lovely woman … I am sorry.

PHIL: Of course! Don't worry, dear. I have a question, but please tell me the truth, OK?

ANNE: Yes, of course!

PHIL: Would you like to work for me? I need somebody to assist my customers at the shop, and I much prefer women, since they are very careful with the fabric when taking the stock in and out. Most of the time when I have to travel, I need someone there!

ANNE: Really? I can't believe this. I would love to work at your shop. Of course I will!

PHIL: Would you start tomorrow?

ANNE: Yes! I'll be there.

PHIL: Sure thing. I'll be waiting for you in the afternoon.

They hug, and Phil waits for Anne to get inside.

Phil is a tall man in his late fifties with blue eyes, with white skin and well-marked wrinkles, a nice body, and a little belly. He was elegant and cultured, from a family of merchants and tailors with a very good financial situation. He was an interesting man, charming but disillusioned with life.

On the following day, Albertina is naked at Constantino's house, and he's telling her what to do.

CONSTANTINO: Put this cushion between your legs and kneel on the bed … rest your right hand on the wall, and hold this bouquet in front of you … yes, perfect! Now turn your body a little towards me, and with your left hand interlace your hair between your fingers, so that your breast appears amidst your hair. Wow! Let's begin.

Constantino starts painting, and little by little it comes alive: a beautiful painting of a pretty sexy woman. But there is also romanticism, with the shadow coming from the window causing the most natural effects of shade and light over the nude body. Albertina remains in a sensual pose, the bouquet bringing a delicacy to the portrait.

Meanwhile, Anne has come to Mr Phil's store, feeling very happy and ready to learn from the new boss, who is introducing her to the shop and to how everything works. Anne has an expressive face, large caramel-coloured eyes, a full mouth, fair skin, thick eyebrows, and wavy brown hair. She is tall and has well-defined hips, a small waist, and large breasts. She is thirty-five years old, and she is pretty but not delicate and petite like Albertina.

PHIL: Here is the tapestry. It's a good way to gain profit for the shop, so always offer to show it to the customers. The shelf right of the entrance only has silk. The women always look there first. The smoothest and bulkier fabrics are mixed with cotton.

ANNE: They are beautiful …

PHIL: On the left side, we have velvet and satin. These fabrics are used for curtains, to upholster seats and the interiors of carriages.

ANNE: They are really beautiful, especially this Bordeaux velvet with damask shapes!

PHIL: Ah! This one I sold to a big customer, the Earl of Brentshe, Lord Edwin. He is very wealthy and has covered his landau carriage with it—he is the only one to have one. It's made in Germany. He also has a barouche passenger carriage which was made in France. He is always here, you'll meet him.

ANNE: Wow! That's amazing! I want to see how it all works!

CHAPTER

2

THE BUYER

Some days after, at the countryside art fair, Constantino is thrilled to be organizing his stall to exhibit his first painting of Albertina. With arrogance and contempt, he looks at the next stall, showing his friend Frederic that he has a new painting. His friend can only stare. Constantino becomes aggressive towards him.

CONSTANTINO: What's wrong, Frederic? Why are you shocked?

Frederic: Wow! What's this?

CONSTANTINO: A painting, can't you see?

Frederic: Yes … but how did you paint it? Who is this woman?

CONSTANTINO: How? I am a painter, and I have skills! That's all.

FREDERIC: Don't give me that! Where did you find this pretty lady? She is what calls attention to the painting. You didn't do anything extraordinary—just gave life to a beautiful woman … wait a minute, I think I know her!

CONSTANTINO: Stop, Frederic! My job and my stuff are none of your business; you are a jealous man, and you know today I am going to sell this painting.

FREDERIC: I mean it! I think I know her … I don't know … I can't stop looking at her.

CONSTANTINO: No you don't! How could you? She is here inside my mind.

FREDERIC: Ah, Constantino! You are telling me that you have imagined this girl? I am a painter myself …

Many people start gathering around Constantino's stall to see the painting. Everyone starts blabbering about its beauty.

CONSTANTINO: Get out of here, Frederic, you are annoying me. I'll punch your face if you don't shut up!

Frederic backs off and goes back to his stall. People are pushing one another to see the painting, which brings more people.

On the other side of the fair, Lord Edwin and his servant Patrick walk together. The women start whispering amongst themselves as he passes through. Edwin is a wealthy and powerful earl of Brentshe but lives in a beautiful mansion on the farm. He is a handsome man, tall, thin, light-eyed and fair-skinned, with beautiful hair that touched his face. He has a striking smile and dimples on his cheek that make him look beyond standard. He is modest and very kind but very demanding with women.

His friend Oswald sees him from far away.

OSWALD: Look who is coming! Edwin! Edwin!

Oswald raises his hand and goes towards him.

EDWIN: Well, well! If it isn't my dear friend who loves balls and pretty ladies! Weren't you supposed should be at my house giving the dinner guidelines tonight, after all you are my favorite ceremonialist.

OSWALD: Yes, I was supposed to, but you know I can't miss this fair. I love coming here, right?

EDWIN: *(laughs)* Of course I know! You brought me here first, remember? You said, "I'll take you to a place filled with beautiful ladies."

OSWALD: I do. But what are you doing here?

EDWIN: I came to buy some things for my house. I throw away many things! I don't want anything that reminds me of Helena. I need a new life … a new home …

OSWALD: And a new wife … *(laughs)*

EDWIN: Speaking of, how is our guest list for the dinner?

OSWALD: It is great, filled with beautiful ladies! *(laughs)*

EDWIN: Well, it's great to hear that! Thank you, my friend.

Edwin pats Oswald's back and says goodbye.

OSWALD: All right then, I'll see you later!

Edwin keeps walking with Patrick through the fair. When he sees a crowd at Constantino's stall, he walks towards it.

CONSTANTINO: This painting reveals the feminine soul with its mystery, sweetness, and charm!

A gentleman approaches.

CONSTANTINO: Does the gentleman want to take a closer look? please, let him come …

GENTLEMAN: how much?

Constantino discloses the price. Everyone is astonished, and some are whispering, "Very expensive!"

Lord Edwin, known as one of the wealthiest people in the city, approaches.

EDWIN: What's happening here? Why is it so crowded?

People are talking amongst themselves: "The earl of Brentshe, is here!" "He can buy it." "Make way."

Lord Edwin comes closer to the painting.

EDWIN: Wow!

For some moments of silence, Edwin admires the painting, looking closer then stepping back. Constantino mingles in the crowd and just watches.

EDWIN: Who is the painter?

CONSTANTINO: I am, sir! Constantino.

EDWIN: Nice to meet you, Constantino.

CONSTANTINO: You too, Lord Edwin.

EDWIN: Tell me about this artwork!

CONSTANTINO: This painting reveals the feminine soul with its mystery, sweetness and charm! The bouquet discloses a scented woman with beautiful roses from the richest gardens in England. Her hair gently touches her waist, bringing our eyes to her hips, making us imagine …

"How absurd!" says a woman. "Outrageous," says another. Little by little the women start taking their husbands away. The place becomes empty.

EDWIN: I'll buy it! What do you think, Patrick?

PATRICK: Yes, no doubt, it's a beautiful painting. In fact, she's a very compelling lady with a unique look.

EDWIN: Unique look … yes, you are right. The painter hasn't talked about her look.

CONSTANTINO: I was just going to, but that woman didn't let me finish!

EDWIN: Well then, go on, my dear man. I want to know every single detail of this work, and I do mean everything, since there aren't any women around us to interrupt. I want to know more about this nude body!

CONSTANTINO: Ah, this naked and compelling body … what to say about its sharp look, searching for something … and its delicate hands pulling the hair, revealing the full breasts, expressing feminine beauty and making us imagine …

EDWIN: Yes, it makes us wonder … all right, I'll take it! But tell me, who is this lady?

Edwin pays Constantino.

CONSTANTINO: She comes from my imagination …

Constantino closes his eyes, as if searching his thoughts.

EDWIN: Then imagine more, for I want two more pictures of her, in different positions and other angles. I will be back!

Edwin leaves with Patrick, who carries the portrait. Constantino is very happy with the money he has made, waving as they depart.

Constantino was abandoned by his father as a child. His mother was a seamstress and a thief. She used to steal from her own customers and sold their belongings at a low price to illegal traders. Having been abandoned by his father and neglected and unloved by his mother, he grew up angry, aggressive, and of bad character. Constantino is twenty-eight years old and of average attractiveness for the typical Englishman. He is slim and tall, and has a big nose, brown eyes, and long brown hair that he always wears in a ponytail.

When Edwin gets home with his servant Patrick, he sees his best friend Oswald talking to his housekeeper, Maria, about the dinner party to be held at Edwin's mansion. These parties were supposed to help Lord Edwin meet a pretty lady and remarry. He has recently lost his wife and is feeling such a deep sorrow that he didn't want to do anything. However, Oswald, who was a womanizer, couldn't understand his friend for not wanting to party or meet new women. That's why Oswald has been insisting on helping his friend keep an active social life and is always organizing dinners.

But Edwin, besides being a gentleman of indisputable beauty, is a simple man with a good heart. He never thinks of women as objects or something to be used, and he would never take advantage of such beliefs. His personality is much more romantic, a man willing to have a family. He was searching for only one woman to please him.

Oswald and Maria, the housekeeper, are talking about what to serve for dinner.

EDWIN: *(whispering aside to Patrick)* Take the painting to my bedroom, I don't want Oswald to see it.

PATRICK: Yes, sir!

OSWALD: … roasted rabbit with potatoes and wine gravy … to start, melon with ham … and at the end of the dinner, we can impress our guests with café au lait, coffee and milk, which is not very known yet!

MARIA: Yes, Mr Oswald, we have all of that here! To decorate the table and match with our menu, what do you think of purple orchids?

OSWALD: Yes, perfect to stimulate the ladies! *(laughs)*

EDWIN: Have you come to an agreement?

MARIA: Yes! Oswald is lovely and has a very good taste.

EDWIN: Don't be modest, my dear Maria! He doesn't know anything, all he does is order. You are the boss here. *(laughs)* I bet he orders duck!

OSWALD: Not even close! I asked for rabbit.

They laugh.

EDWIN: You're going to ruin my food pantry

OSWALD: Well, thank you, Maria! I have to go, Edwin. I'll see you at eight for dinner!

Oswald leaves. Maria sets the table. Edwin goes to his bedroom and calls for Patrick.

EDWIN: Patrick! Get that easel and bring it here. Let's put the painting on it and leave it here for now.

Patrick leaves. Edwin stares, amazed at the painting, and caresses Albertina's body on the canvas. A few moments later Patrick returns.

PATRICK: Here you are, my lord! Allow me … there you go. The portrait's perfect there!

EDWIN: Sublime! Wonderful! Thank you, Patrick, I'm going to get some rest and then get ready for dinner.

A violinist plays classical music as Edwin welcomes his guests at the door to the dining room. Some are already known to him and others are being presented for the first time. There are more ladies than gentlemen. Edwin is a very courteous man and makes a point of kissing every woman's hand.

OSWALD: Edwin, I'd like to introduce to you a very special lady! This is Isabel, daughter of Margaret di *Médici*.

Isabel belongs to the very important Médici family. Her mother is Duchess Margaret di Médici and her father Duke James di Medici. A spoiled, prejudiced, and unsympathetic young woman, she is of average beauty, but her way of being overshadows her beauty. She is a beautiful but dull woman, without charm or sweetness, and flaunts her wealth and power. Isabel speaks five languages and has studied at the best schools. She plays the piano and has studied literature at a prestigious university in Paris. With so many attributes, she can choose whom to marry but has fallen in love with the wrong man the coveted Lord Edwin.

EDWIN: You are very welcome to my home, Lady Isabel.

ISABEL: It's my pleasure, Lord Edwin.

EDWIN: And how is your mother? For the next dinner bring her along. The Duchess is a wonderful woman.

Isabel is flattered by this acknowledgement of her mother's prestige, and uses it to get closer to Lord Edwin. She sits next to him at the table, creating a discomfort among the other ladies, who are complaining to Oswald about the lack of opportunities to meet Edwin.

OSWALD: Is everyone comfortable? Lord Edwin and I are very pleased to have you all here. Have the pleasure of tasting these delicacies that were made with love for you. Cheers!

Everyone takes up their glasses, smiling, but Isabel looks to Edwin, who seems to be charmed by a lady, named Laila, on the other side of the table. He gestures to a servant to fill Laila's glass. Isabel notices Laila is looking at Edwin so she interrupts.

ISABEL: Lord Edwin? Don't inebriate the ladies! They say a good gentleman never offers what is forbidden! *(laughs)*

EDWIN: Not quite, my dear! They say a good gentleman always inebriates the ladies, and lets them burn in desire!

They all laugh. The dinner proceeds naturally, and little by little some people leave. Few are left, around six people, among them Isabel, Oswald, and Laila, all a bit drunk.

LAILA: Hey! Miss? Is he your boyfriend?

ISABEL: What? Who? No!

LAILA: So why you can't just let his leg go? Come sit by me so we can talk.

Isabel is visibly shaken. She does take Laila's offense and replies rudely.

ISABEL: Just by looking at you, I know there won't be any good conversation between us. I would rather listen to a man's gallantries than waste my time with a hysterical girl like you.

They all fall silent. Isabel says goodbye to Edwin and Oswald, a carriage with her servant waiting outside . After some minuts the guests all leave.

On the following day, Constantino wakes up feeling lively and gets dressed to go to Albertina's house, in the expectation of making more money with the girl, two more paintings having already been commissioned. When Constantino arrives, he pounds on the door, calling for Albertina, who opens the door slightly and peers through the gap, alarmed.

Albertina: What is it, Constantino?

Adele watches Constantino talk with Albertina.

Constantino: We need to paint a new portrait! Hurry! Let's go to my house.

Albertina: Why are you in such a hurry? We have just painted one. Sell it first!

Constantino: Yes, we painted one, but nobody wanted it! We shall try others. We need money, don't we?

Albertina: Yes, we do. Wait for me. I'll be on my way.

Albertina shuts the door, and looks at Adele.

Albertina: Missus, can you stay with William for me, please?

Adele: Yes, my dear. But why is he in a hurry, if he hasn't sold other paintings yet? That's odd, don't you think?

Albertina: Yes, I'm puzzled too. But I have to go. I won't be long.

Albertina goes back to the house with Constantino. When they get there, they do not even talk. She takes off her clothes. Constantino instructs her.

Constantino: Please, lie down on the sofa, facing down. Hug the cushion and bring your knee towards your belly.

She obeys. He looks at her and begins painting her for the second time.

Meanwhile, Edwin is sitting on the edge of his bed, looking at Albertina's portrait. Patrick knocks on the door.

EDWIN: Come in!

PATRICK: I brought you some food. You haven't got up yet … we are worried about you!

EDWIN: Do you know what? Those dinners are not worth it. I never get to know any woman who would truly please me! How is that possible? Oswald keeps doing it to please me, poor fellow …

PATRICK: I understand, my lord. That's why I never leave the town's saloon. *(laughs)* It's much more fun.

EDWIN: *(laughs)* I see … wait! I have an idea. Can you bring me a prostitute?

PATRICK: Sure I can! Do you want her now?

EDWIN: Yes, and until I can fulfil my hunger! By the time you take her back, it will be nightfall. Go! Hurry!

PATRICK: All right, I am on my way.

Two Hours later, Patrick knocks on Edwin's door.

EDWIN: Come in! Hello! Nice to meet you. I'm Edwin. And you, miss? What's your name?

CATHARINA: Catharina, sir.

Edwin doesn't waste time. He is thirsty for sex. He takes off Catharina's clothes and consumes her eagerly. One Hours later, she walks to carriage where Patrick is waiting for her.

Although the time with the prostitute was good, Edwin is really looking to find love and have a family. He is trying to forget everything that reminds him of his late wife. The house is a little messy. Edwin asks for Maria to oversee disposing of some of his things and donating other things that had belonged to his deceased wife, Helena.

EDWIN: I don't want this anymore …

MARIA: Oh, My Lord, but this mirror is so beautiful!

EDWIN: Take it for yourself! I am not interested in the image of that saint, it was Helena's … I don't want anything that reminds of her. It's torture.

MARIA: Yes, you are right, of course.

EDWIN: This corner table I have given to Patrick. He'll take it today. And that dressing table in my room is for you.

MARIA: My lord, if you don't mind, I would like to give the dressing table to my daughter.

EDWIN: Of course! And how is she? Has her husband quit drinking?

MARIA: She is fine! But he hasn't stopped completely …

PATRICK: My lord, the carriage is ready. We may go whenever you want.

EDWIN: That's all for today, Maria, thank you. We'll finish this later. I've got go to Mr Phil's shop.

Edwin and Patrick leave the house and get into the carriage. On their way, there are beautiful trees, and the sun is shining. Edwin only thinks of Albertina, remembers her image in the painting with a heart full of hope to make this love real. Edwin can have any woman he wants, in addition to his beauty and charisma, he is a desired and well-known man in the village. But he didn't meet anyone who stirred his heart. Albertina's painting stirred his thoughts. Albertina, in addition to being beautiful, has a sweet face, a sexy body and striking eyes.

CHAPTER

3

THE ENVY

Margaret di Médice enters Mr. Phil's shop with her daughter Isabel, Mr Phil approaches Margaret.

PHIL: Well, well, look who is here! My favourite client! How have you been, Your Grace? How about you, my lady Isabel? Anne, this is the Duchess Margaret di Médici and her daughter, Lady Isabel.

ANNE: Nice to meet you, Your Grace!

MARGARET: Likewise, my dear! It's nice to have you here to assist us.

Mr Phil steps off to show Isabel a fabric, Margaret whispering to Anne.

MARGARET: Glad you're keeping Mister Phil company... and helping him. He didn't deserve what happened.

ANNE: What?

Isabel calls her mother and interrupts the conversation.

ISABEL: Mother! Come and see this satin.

MARGARET: Yes, it's beautiful. But I do not prefer this colour … it's a very strong blue.

ISABEL: Well, I like it. It's different. I'll take it.

MARGARET: Anne! Please help me here. Show me what's new.

ANNE: Of course. Let's begin with silk. Come! We have this one in "intense rouge"; this one, with the pearl glow mixed with French lace. That would be an amazing dress!

ISABEL: What a disgrace! It will look like a nightgown … *(laughs)*

MARGARET: Isabel! That's rude. It isn't funny … stop now.

ISABEL: I apologize! It is very delicate, this. I like strong and bright colours, audacious perhaps … black is rather popular, though strong.

PHIL: Here it is! Tea for the ladies.

ISABEL: Thank you, Mr Phil. I really needed this.

Margaret gets her tea and sips it cheerfully.

PHIL: Anne my dear, this is for you!

Isabel whispers to her mother.

ISABEL: What an insult. He wants his maid to have tea with us.

MARGARET: Shut your dirty mouth! If you ever shame me again, you can say bye-bye to your trip. I won't give you a penny.

Edwin enters the shop with Patrick.

EDWIN: What is this? A party, and I haven't been invited? *(laughs)*

They all look at one another, laughing. Phil rushes to greet him, and Isabel's eyes shine, seeking a new opportunity to get closer to Edwin again.

PHIL: Edwin! Join us. What would you like to drink?

EDWIN: Wine.

EDWIN: Duchess, how have you been?

MARGARET: I am fine. And you, my dear?

EDWIN: Fine too, thank you. And you, Lady … Isabel?

Edwin kisses her hand.

ISABEL: I am fantastic!

PHIL: Edwin, this is my new employee, Anne.

EDWIN: Oh, well! Great news, then! It's a pleasure to meet you, Anne!

Edwin kisses her hand. Isabel looks with contempt and interrupts.

ISABEL: What brings you here, Lord Edwin?

As he walks through the shop with his glass of wine, he sees on the counter the pearl silk with French lace that Anne had shown to Margaret.

EDWIN: How beautiful these fabrics are … so delicate! They would make a beautiful dress.

MARGARET: I'll take them!

ISABEL: You haven't said anything …

EDWIN: I came to buy some fabric for new curtains. Anne, what do you suggest? I don't want blue …

He steps away with disdain from the blue fabric Isabel was going to buy.

ANNE: We have a moss green mixed with khaki, and pearl mixed with bordeaux …

EDWIN: I like the second one, but I will look a little more. Patrick? I want your opinion.

Edwin goes around the shop with Patrick while Phil gives him full attention. Isabel tries to tag along with them. Anne has the opportunity to be with Margaret alone.

ANNE: Duchess?

MARGARET: Yes, dear?

ANNE: What did you mean earlier? What wasn't fair? What happened to Mr Phil?

MARGARET: Please don't say anything to him about this conversation, but his wife ran away with an employee from the shop. It was a disaster in his life. The shop was closed for a week. It was the talk of the town.

ANNE: Oh my god!

Anne puts her hands over her mouth.

MARGARET: I am very glad that he found you. You will be good company for him and good help in the shop.

ANNE: Yes, thank you for telling me.

PHIL: Anne? Cut Lord Edwin's fabric.

Anne goes to assist along with Phil. Isabel gets closer to Edwin without anyone noticing and whispers to him.

ISABEL: Lord Edwin? There will be a dinner at my house, and I'd like you to come! Will the gentleman give me the honour?

Edwin: I appreciate the invitation, Lady, but I have a lot of commitments in the next few weeks, and it's not a good time for me to have fun. I hope your dinner is wonderful and that you are in good company.

Phil: Here it is, Lord Edwin.

Edwin: Thank you, I'll see you later.

Edwin says goodbye to everyone.

CHAPTER

4

THE HOPE

A few days pass. While Constantino is mixing the colours and preparing to paint the third painting, Albertina gets distracted by looking around his house and sees his second painting, which is already finished in the corner of the house. She walks slowly, with a curious look, until she touches the painting. She stares, amazed by her own portrait, sliding her hand over the canvas, feeling the texture and perfection of the painting. Her thoughts are vague but she wonders to herself in a low voice that Constantino overhears.

Albertina: Who would buy this portrait?

She strokes the frame.

Constantino: I don't know … it is hard to sell.

Albertina: Calm down! You have exhibited it only once, of course you will sell it! If I had the money, I would buy it.

Constantino: *(laughs)* Of course! It's you. Everyone wants their own painting! I can't stand painting portraits of those annoying noblemen.

Albertina listens, spreading sandalwood oil on her hands. She spills a drop on the picture unintentionally, right on the corner, and tries to clean it quickly so Constantino doesn't see it.

ALBERTINA: What kind of paintings do you make the most? Landscapes, people, still lifes, flowers?

CONSTANTINO: I am not a well-known painter yet, so I've ended up painting portraits. I would like to paint female nudes and nature.

ALBERTINA: Have you got a wife?

CONSTANTINO: No!

ALBERTINA: Have you been married? Would you like to be?

CONSTANTINO: You are asking a lot of questions, don't you think?

ALBERTINA: No.

CONSTANTINO: Well, let's begin. Sit on the sofa. Now turn onto your side and raise your left leg, bent. Put your hand near your knee, bend your body into the sofa, and with your right hand hold your breast. Look at me—

The sun sets, and night comes. Mr. Phil locks the shop door and then goes to put the money in the safe at the back of the shop. He calls to Anne.

PHIL: I'll be right there to help you.

When he returns, Anne is on the ladder putting some fabric on the shelf. Phil steps behind a rack and inspects Anne's body. He gets closer as if to help her, and she is startled and almost falls. Phil catches her and holds her hands as they look at each other.

PHIL: Be careful! But I'll catch you …

ANNE: You scared me, Mr Phil!

She was a little embarrassed.

PHIL: You don't have to call me mister, my dear.

ANNE: Thank you, Phil! Well, I am done tidying up the shop. And you, Mr Phil? *(laughs)* I'm sorry. Phil, what do you do after closing the shop?

PHIL: Well … I go upstairs, where I live. I have a glass of wine and rest. Sometimes a friend comes to see me, and we play cards and talk.

ANNE: Having friends is wonderful …

PHIL: Would you like to have a glass of wine with me, and talk for a while?

ANNE: I'd love to!

They go upstairs where Phil lives, and Anne seems to feel safe and comfortable with her boss. After Margaret di Médici told her about Phil being abandoned by his wife for a shop employee, she has felt she wanted to get closer to him.

PHIL: Sit down, dear. Here, this is for you, and this is for me. Cheers!

ANNE: Thank you, Phil … for everything! I am very glad to be working here with you, having you close to me.

PHIL: I am glad I found you too … in fact, I'd like to thank that lady for bringing you here the other day. *(laughing)* I can't remember her name.

ANNE: Oh yes! Albertina, but I don't know her … the other day she went away so fast that I couldn't even ask for her name. Sometimes I think about her … she was so good to me, I will never forget her.

PHIL: True. She was really brave … fortunately, nothing more has happened to you.

They look at each other, speechless. Anne smiles.

PHIL: You have a beautiful smile!

ANNE: Thank you!

They look at each other, again retreating into wordlessness.

ANNE: Well … I have to go.

PHIL: Of course, my dear. I will walk you home!

They leave the shop and walk with linked arms until they reach Anne's house.

ANNE: Here we are!

She teeters off balance and holds Phil's shoulder, laughing. He holds onto her hips, and their bodies come closer. They look at each other, and Phil kisses her.

Anne's mother, Margot, is watching through the window as Anne says goodbye and comes into the house. Her mother looks to her with anger.

MARGOT: Who was that?

ANNE: My boss, Mr Phil.

MARGOT: And when it was time to say goodbye, you kissed him?

Anne stares her mother, sadly.

MARGOT: You have just got this job … aren't you ashamed of acting like a whore?

ANNE: I didn't do anything! He kissed me.

MARGOT: But you allowed him, you pervert. Do you really think he likes you? *(laughs)* He will use you and leave you, just like the other.

ANNE: No, we don't know that! You will have to wait and see if your wishes come true.

MARGOT: It is not a wish. I am only saying it because I want you well … I don't want you to suffer again.

ANNE: I am tired. I am going to bed.

Anne goes upstairs. Margot calls after her, and Anne looks back.

MARGOT: Anne! Has he got any money?

ANNE: What's the difference, if he will only use me and leave me?

Margot stares at Anne. She turns and goes to her room.

Margot is a bitter woman, and she is jealous of her daughter. She doesn't want to see anyone happy. Deep down, she knows she will always be alone. She has never been able to find great love, but she has gone through betrayal and abandonment. She doesn't leave the house, and she doesn't have friends. She wants her daughter to remain single and by her side.

Margot lives on the money from renting out a tavern that she inherited from her father. She doesn't have to work, and she lives in a good house that she also inherited from her father. He passed away leaving just her and Anne, but the money was enough to live on.

Some days later, Constantino is settling his portraits in his stall. He puts a SOLD sign on them. Frederic approaches.

FREDERIC: More portraits of the beautiful lady! How is she?

CONSTANTINO: I am tired, Frederic. Please just leave me alone.

FREDERIC: I bet you didn't give a penny to this young lady, just as you do with the rest.

CONSTANTINO: It's none of your business.

Edwin approaches with Patrick and heads straight to the paintings of Albertina.

EDWIN: My paintings! They are ready. Great!

CONSTANTINO: Yes! I rushed to deliver them. Do you like them?

EDWIN: Yes, she is still beautiful! Look at her hair … her skin white as snow. Her eyes … they are the most beautiful eyes I have ever seen. What do you think, Patrick?

PATRICK: They are really nice. I like them a lot.

CONSTANTINO: Beyond her beauty is the delicacy of this portrait. A masterpiece! Observe the finishing elements on the frame, made of the noble wood jacaranda!

EDWIN: I hadn't noticed the frame *(laughs)* … it's fancy, indeed.

PATRICK: I noticed. It is very fine. And you, Constantino—where do you live? In the town, or around here?

CONSTANTINO: Me? I live in the village near here.

Frederic stares and nods his head while Constantino tells him lies.

EDWIN: Do you live with anyone? Have you got a wife and children?

CONSTANTINO: I live on my own. I haven't got a wife or children.

EDWIN: I see … well, how much do I own you?

Constantino gives the price, and it's higher than the first one. Edwin is displeased.

EDWIN: Are you mad? That's absurd! I ordered two more, and you want to extort me?

CONSTANTINO: No! Not at all. I am just offering the very best for you, My Lord. I have done what you've asked and even added a noble wood frame … I am just a painter, Lord Edwin. Please do not think badly of me. Besides, you will be the only collector of the artwork known as "living painting".

Edwin grabs Constantino's collar and shouts in his ears.

Edwin: So tell me, who is this lady!

Patrick holds Edwin as Constantino gets scared. Frederick is staring.

Constantino: She is not real. I am so sorry.

Edwin: Liar!

Constantino: No! I would never lie. Why would I do that?

Edwin looks at Constantino, a little confused but seeming to believe.

Edwin: All right, here is the money! I'd like to order another one.

Constantino: An order? What will it be? One more portrait …

Edwin: Yes! But with another lady, as beautiful as this one.

Constantino is surprised and does not know how to answer.

Constantino: Another girl? Hmm … I don't know … let me think! You don't want it with the same one?

Edwin: *(laughs)* It was just a joke … of course I want the same girl. But this time, I want her seated on the front door wrapped in a bedsheet.

Constantino: All right …

Edwin: I will be back.

Edwin walks away with Patrick and his two paintings. Frederick follows them, unnoticed.

Frederic: Lord Edwin? Your Lordship—

Edwin stops and look back.

FREDERIC: I am pretty sure that the girl in the painting is real!

EDWIN: You think? Why?

FREDERIC: He does not do this kind of portrait without a woman posing for him. He is a specialist of portraits, and besides he is a great liar.

EDWIN: Oh, I see … thanks for telling me. But do you know how can I find out more about this girl?

FREDERIC: He never tells me about his life, and as I said, he lies to everyone. But I know that he lives in town, and perhaps she is from there.

EDWIN: Yes, I am sure you are right. I should think about that. What do you think, Patrick?

PATRICK: I agree with this gentleman, I myself have assumed that Constantino lies all the time. He would not be able to invent such a woman.

EDWIN: All right, I appreciate it! We will talk later.

CHAPTER

5

THE BRIDE

After a long, hard workday, Anne and Mr. Phil are ready to close the shop and start organizing everything.

The door is locked, and Phil counts the money before putting it in the safe, as he does every day. However, he is feeling a bit anxious to talk to Anne about having a relationship. He is afraid of scaring her off, but at the same time he is in love with her and wants to end his affliction.

PHIL: I am exhausted! It was a busy day today.

ANNE: Is it always like that when the goods arrive?

PHIL: Yes always, there's a lot to organize. You see how I need you here with me. *(chuckles)* How are you, my darling?

ANNE: I am fine. *(laughs)* I enjoyed learning about the goods' arrival, how to organize them, and how to show them to customers.

Phil gives Anne a serious look and puts his hand on her shoulders.

PHIL: Anne, I need to talk to you. Can you stay a little longer? I will walk you home later.

ANNE: Yes, of course! What has happened?

Anne looks at Phil's eyes, worried and not knowing what he is going to say. In her head many thoughts are coming and going, especially after everything her mother said. Margot is a terrible mother to Anne, a bitter woman who always gets in her way, as has become very clear to Anne as time passed.

Anne is afraid of losing her job, since she got it so recently, and she has no clue of what Mr. Phil wants to talk to her about. Anne has lost faith in people, as there have been too many disappointments in her life.

PHIL: Well, let's go upstairs and talk. Would you like something to drink?

Anne nods, and they go upstairs. Phil takes two wine glasses and pours them both.

PHIL: Cheers! Anne, I know it is too early to tell you this. We've known each other just for a short while. But I am very fond of you, and after yesterday I was sure …

Anne gazes fixedly at Phil and listens intently.

PHIL: I want to know if you would marry me, and together we will start a new life. I have liked you since the very first moment I saw you. Working with you at the shop, I see how dedicated you are … and after our kiss, I can't stay here alone, without you …

Anne looks in his eyes, in love, and smiles.

ANNE: Yes! Oh my, I'm surprised! Everything happens so fast. I really want to be with you, Phil. My life took on real meaning after we first met and I started working here. I love being with you.

They kiss. He holds her in his arms.

PHIL: *(whispering)* It's great to know that. I am very happy to have you.

Phil steps back.

PHIL: Close your eyes. I want to give you something.

Phil gets a ring and puts it on Anne's finger.

PHIL: Anne, you are now my fiancée.

Anne is amazed by her gift.

ANNE: My god, it is breathtaking! I am so happy.

PHIL: Soon, we'll get married. You will live here and take care of the business with me.

They kiss, madly in love.

ANNE: I am very happy and so fond of you! I love you!

PHIL: I love you too.

Phil kisses her hands.

PHIL: Shall we? I'll walk you home.

Phil and Anne walk through the streets until they almost reach Anne's house.

ANNE: Let's stop here, before we get to my house, so my mother won't see us through the window. She is jealous. I'll tell her about us little by little. I will tell her later you proposed to me.

PHIL: I see …

Phil says goodbye to Anne and walks back home.

Nearby, Constantino is walking down the street. He enters a brothel with a bit of arrogance, since he has a lot of money to spend on drinks and women. After playing and drinking with the other clients of the whorehouse, Constantino is very high and a little aggressive. He goes up to a bedroom with a prostitute named Catharina, the same woman who was at Lord Edwin's house. He is not seeking sex but wants to torture the girl. She screams and shouts for help.

CONSTANTINO: Shut up, bitch! Come here! You whore, I am paying you to obey me.

CATHARINA: Stop! Don't do this … help! I need to breathe, let me go!

Catharina escapes from under Constantino and runs towards the door. He pulls her back in and punches her in the face.

In the corridor, other customers leave their rooms and run to stop the fight. One of them punches Constantino. They throw him out of the brothel. Others help Catharina, whose nose is bleeding.

Meanwhile, Edwin has set up his new portraits in his bedroom with Patrick's help.

EDWIN: They're great just like this. I'll leave them here in the bedroom, until the hall is ready. Thank you. Patrick, that's all for today.

PATRICK: Call if you need me.

Edwin is alone in his bedroom, seated on the edge of his bed, as he treasures his portraits. Now there are three. He starts to drink and thinks aloud.

EDWIN: Does she really exist?

Edwin stares fixedly at one of his paintings and walks towards it. He rubs a hand over it.

EDWIN: The most beautiful girl I've ever seen …

As he draws close to the painting, he smells the sandalwood oil which Albertina had spilled. He sniffs the painting trying to locate the source of the sandalwood. He smells the other paintings but realizes they don't all have sandalwood in the paint—only the one.

EDWIN: So this scent can't be coming from the painter! It could belong to a woman, of course! And only one painting has the smell …

Edwin drinks more and gets higher.

EDWIN: Now I am sure you are real, and I won't give up until I find you.

He sits on the bed again, staring at the painting, so drunk he can barely sit up. He starts to hallucinate about being with Albertina in the painting. He sees the images moving, he reaches his hand to meet her hand … then his body falls back onto the bed, and he falls asleep.

The next day, Maria, his housekeeper, knocks on the door. Edwin does not answer, so Maria calls for Patrick.

MARIA: Patrick! Please come see to Lord Edwin. It is late, and he does not seem to be awake yet. I knocked his door but he hasn't answered.

PATRICK: Sure, let's go!

Patrick knocks on the door, but Edwin still doesn't answer. The two servants step in and see that he is sleeping. Patrick gets closer to his bed to check if everything is all right.

PATRICK: Lord Edwin?

Edwin slowly wakes up.

EDWIN: My god, what a headache! I am sick … I am finished … a rag … Maria? Help me … water … water …

MARIA: Yes, My Lord, I'll be right back!

PATRICK: But are you all right?

EDWIN: I am terrible, Patrick. I am in love, and I don't know this girl … I need to find her!

PATRICK: I understand … I want to help you, but what can I do?

Maria returns to the room.

MARIA: Here, water … food … you need to eat.

EDWIN: Thank you!

Out in the hallway, the voice of Edwin's friend Oswald is heard.

OSWALD: Hello? Hello?

Oswald spots Maria through the doorway.

MARIA: Hello, Mr Oswald!

OSWALD: What's this? What's happening here? Why are you in bed, Edwin? what about our dinner?

EDWIN: Yes, I know. There will be no dinner. I am sorry, my friend … I can't.

OSWALD: What have you got?

EDWIN: Tell him, Patrick!

PATRICK: Lord Edwin is in love.

OSWALD: Is that so? Well, this is good news! Who is the lady?

Edwin nods towards the paintings, and Oswald moves closer to look at them.

OSWALD: Are you joking? Edwin, are you serious? You're in love with a painting?

EDWIN: Yes … help me find her.

OSWALD: Poor you! I've never seen you like this … well, let me see how can I help you.

MARIA: Yes, poor you, My Lord.

PATRICK: We'll find her. It's just a matter of time.

They all look at Edwin in bed, not knowing what to do.

Outside Constantino's house, Albertina is wrapped in a bedsheet, seated on the front steps. Constantino is painting his fourth portrait.

CONSTANTINO: This time, I will sell it at a new fair. I don't want to depend only on that one.

ALBERTINA: Why?

CONSTANTINO: Well, because … I will try.

ALBERTINA: I can help if you want! I can stay at the usual fair with two of the paintings, and you can go to the other with two more.

Constantino looks at her, taken by surprise, as he doesn't have the other portraits and wouldn't want her to be seen in public with them.

CONSTANTINO: Are you mad? Absolutely not! Thank you, but it won't be necessary.

Constantino continues to paint his picture.

A few days later, Albertina is sleeping as Adele calls her quietly.

ADELE: Albertina? Albertina?

ALBERTINA: Hello, Mrs Adele!

ADELE: Dear, it is very early, but I am going to work for my sister. She is a nanny and cares for the child of a well-to-do family. She is too ill to be by herself. We'll talk later.

ALBERTINA: I am really sorry for your sister!

They say goodbye.

At the smaller art fair, Constantino is exhibiting his new painting, thinking out loud as he sets up.

CONSTANTINO: Today is my lucky day. I think I will do well here. I am fed up with depending on that snobbish earl to buy my portraits.

Adele walks by, tending the child of the couple who are her sister's employers. They stop at Constantino's stall as the couple stares at the paintings. In the midst of some paintings, Albertina's painting stands out.

ADOLF: Beautiful painting, young man! What is your name?

CONSTANTINO: Constantino! Thank you.

ADOLF: This portrait is very interesting. A girl sitting in the door-frame waiting for something! How much is it?

Constantino says the price, and everyone is surprised at how very expensive it is.

ADOLF: That is a very significant amount, my lad. You do know that?

CONSTANTINO: Yes, I do! But I have already sold others.

ADOLF: I like it very much, but I'll pay only half! What do you say? This fair doesn't attract many people willing to pay what you have asked for.

CONSTANTINO: I am sorry, sir, but I can't sell it for any other price.

ADOLF: But I am offering a great deal.

CONSTANTINO: My artwork is worth more.

ADOLF: All right, my lad, good luck!

The family and Adele walk away. Of course, Adele knows who Constantino and Albertina are, but she is silent the whole time.

Edwin walks alone towards Mr. Phil's shop. Looking down, his face sad, he was thinking about his chances of meeting the girl in the painting. He doesn't even know if she exists, but his passion drives him to hold on to his hopes. As he enters the shop, he sees Mr. Phil smiling as never before.

PHIL: Hello, Lord Edwin. Come and join us!

EDWIN: Oh my! It's been a long time since I saw a smile on your face. Mr Phil, what's happening?

PHIL: I have good news. Let's drink, and I'll tell you. Let's go to the costumer's room, the couch is more comfortable, I want to tell you how happy I am.

EDWIN: I want to know everything!

PHIL: Sit down! So—you have followed my life the past few years, and you've seen what I've been through …

EDWIN: Yes, you are a strong man, Phil. I admire you. I don't know if I'd live after that.

PHIL: I know … I don't know how I was able to bear so much pain and shame! But everything has gone by quickly, and I am very happy now, in a way I could not have imagined.

EDWIN: Tell me what's happening! Are you in love?

PHIL: Yes! I'm in love, and I will marry Anne!

EDWIN: Your new employee? That's amazing. I am thrilled for you.

PHIL: I am very happy, my friend.

EDWIN: I can imagine, but how did you meet Anne?

PHIL: Well, I'll tell you, but I want you to keep it a secret.

EDWIN: Yes, of course! I won't tell anyone.

PHIL: A man tried to rape Anne near the train station, but a young woman which is called Albertina, came upon them just in time. She struck him with a rock and grabbed Anne. They ran away and entered my shop asking for help.

EDWIN: Bastard! Makes me want to beat him.

PHIL: I wanted to, but she begged me to forget it.

EDWIN: How brave this Albertina was, what a strong woman! I like women with attitude. But … where is this girl?

PHIL: She went away after leaving Anne here, and we lost contact with her. Anne thinks of her often and wants to thank her, but she doesn't know where Albertina lives.

EDWIN: So you invited Anne to work with you, you spent more time together, and now you are getting married?

PHIL: Yes, we are very happy!

EDWIN: *(laughing)* Very good! Congratulations. And now I need your help with some fabric, I want to cover the wall with one that matches the other I took for the curtains.

PHIL: Yes, let's go! Anne? Come help us! Any fabric that could match the one Lord Edwin took for the curtains?

ANNE: Hello, Lord Edwin. Well, we are waiting for new merchandise and only have the same fabric you have already seen. I suggest you wait for the new arrivals.

EDWIN: All right, I'll wait. I suppose there is nothing here, indeed.

PHIL: As soon as they arrive, I'll bring some samples to show you.

EDWIN: Thank you, Phil. I'll see you later!

They shake hands, and Edwin leaves.

CHAPTER

6

THE INFORMANT

At night, Patrick is drunk, walking down the street with a prostitute. He sees Constantino entering his house.

Patrick: Wait! See that man? I know him!

Prostitute: Yes, that's Constantino. Bastard! He uses women to pose for him and then doesn't give them a penny.

Patrick: You know him, then—he lives here?

Prostitute: Yes, he lives alone.

They stop in front of Constantino's house, and Patrick watches, thinking about everything to come now that he know where Constantine lives. Albertina must be close by, and his boss will be happy with the news.

The night passed and the next day .As the sun is setting, Patrick waits at Edwin's house. Soon Edwin arrives.

Patrick: Lord Edwin! How are you doing? I have been waiting since this morning because I need to talk to you.

Edwin: I was at Oswald's house. I am fine, but I would be better if I had any clue about the lady in the portraits.

Patrick: I see … *(laughs)*

EDWIN: What happened? Why are you so happy?

PATRICK: I am thrilled! Yesterday, I went out and had a lot of fun. On my way back, I saw Constantino.

EDWIN: So what?

PATRICK: Well, now I know where the bastard lives. He lied. He lives in town near the train station and market street.

Edwin looks at Patrick with surprise. He is overjoyed that now, with this new information about Constantino, he may be closer to finding his passion.

EDWIN: I don't believe this! *(laughs)* You are unbelievable, Patrick! Get the horses ready. We are going there!

Adele runs into her house, terrified. Albertina has no idea what's going to happen and how her life will change. Adele's news will break Albertina's heart, but Mrs. Adele is also going through some rough moments because her sister is dying.

ADELE: Albertina! Hello, dear. I'm afraid I don't bring good news. We need to talk.

ALBERTINA: What happened? Your sister—?

ADELE: Yes, my sister. She is dying, the children are sad … they can barely eat … the house is a mess …

ALBERTINA: I am really sad! I don't know what to say.

ADELE: But darling, I am worried about you! Suddenly, everything has changed. I'll have to give this house back today!

ALBERTINA: Oh my goodness! Why will you have to give it back today?

ADELE: Yes, I am leaving to live in her house. So, you know, I pay rent every week. I asked the property administrator to leave you here for a few days, but they won't allow it. They will place a sign today, and tomorrow there's someone to see the house.

ALBERTINA: I am breathless, Mrs Adele! I don't know what to do.

ADELE: I am thinking about who might be able to help you …

ALBERTINA: Don't you worry, Mrs Adele, I will figure this out.

ADELE: Of course I am worried, my dear. I am really fond of you and William—you are like family to me. I will miss you.

Adele watches William play on the floor.

ALBERTINA: I want to thank you for everything you have done for me. I will never forget you …

Albertina hugs Adele, her eyes filled with tears.

ADELE: I wanted to do so much more … but I can't! I am sure you will find somebody, a man who will take of you and William.

They both look at William.

ALBERTINA: It all feels impossible …

ADELE: What? What are you talking about?

ALBERTINA: Life … it seems impossible to have a normal one, basic things I do not have.

ADELE: I understand, Albertina, but soon everything will change, I am sure. You have to believe. I can try to ask somebody to shelter you … I am thinking of someone …

Albertina and Adele clasp hands.

ALBERTINA: Don't worry, I'll fix it. You have done a lot for me. I appreciate it. I know whom to ask for help.

ADELE: Do you mind telling me whom you will ask?

ALBERTINA: I will ask somebody from the market, someone who perhaps has a job for me. I don't want you to worry.

ADELE: Yes! I haven't thought about the folks from the market. Someone will certainly help you.

They both have a smile on their face, and yet Adele looks worried.

ADELE: Albertina, I need to tell you something. It's about Constantino.

ALBERTINA: Constantino? What?

ADELE: I was at the art fair in the village with my sister's employers, and I saw Constantino exhibiting his paintings. One of them was you wrapped in a bed sheet. I didn't see the others with you naked …

ALBERTINA: What's wrong about that?

ADELE: Well, my dear, Lord Adolf, my sister's employer, stopped to look at your painting. I was paying attention, and of course Constantino doesn't know me. When Constantino gave the price, we were shocked at how high it was.

ALBERTINA: That's why he doesn't sell them! He is too greedy …

ADELE: No, Adolf said he would buy the portrait for half the price quoted, but Constantino wouldn't accept it because, he said, he had already sold all the others as at prices like that.

Albertina is shocked hearing this.

ALBERTINA: I can't believe—my goodness, he has been deceiving me all this time! He is always telling me he couldn't sell them, that nobody wanted them.

ADELE: I know, my dear, I am very upset. You do not deserve this.

Hatred consumes Albertina, and it shows on her face.

ALBERTINA: I will talk to that bastard. Things can't go on like this. What is he thinking? That I will just be here to serve him? Mrs Adele, I am going to him right now. I'll be back soon to get my things and William.

ADELE: Yes, darling, I'll wait for you!

Albertina leaves quickly and furiously. It's sunset. She rushes through the streets to Constantino's house. She shouts his name and pounds on the door until Constantino opens it.

ALBERTINA: How could you do this to me? Deceive me for all this time? You're a prick, you do not fear God.

CONSTANTINO: *(imitating Albertina's voice to mock her)* How could you do this to me? Deceive me for all this time? You're a prick, you do not fear god.

ALBERTINA: I am not kidding! You will pay everything you own me.

CONSTANTINO: I have no money!

ALBERTINA: How haven't you got any money? You have sold all three paintings!

CONSTANTINO: I've spent it all!

ALBERTINA: You ask a fortune for each painting … I know you have the money, give it to me now!

CONSTANTINO: You are wrong, my dear! I don't have anything. I've told you. I have spent it all.

ALBERTINA: Why haven't you done as we've agreed? You said you would pay me when you had them sold.

CONSTANTINO: I never said I would pay you … you imagined that.

ALBERTINA: Are you mad? Or only pretending you are?

CONSTANTINO: I haven't promised any money. You asked me about money when we started, and I told you it was difficult to sell a painting. I didn't say I would pay you.

ALBERTINA: You placed an advertisement, and you think the person who answers it must serve you? You don't think you have to pay?

CONSTANTINO: I don't think about it …

Albertina gets furious and attacks Constantino, shouting.

ALBERTINA: Give me my money! Give me my money!

Constantino slaps Albertina on the face, grabs her, opens the door, and throws her into the street. Albertina lies there in the street, scared by the violence and Constantino's threatening attitude. As she is trying to get up, Constantino gets some coins from his pocket and throws them at her, humiliating her even more. He slams the door, and she gets up slowly.

Wandering, she finds the way to her house, but stops to stare at the people sleeping on the street near the train station. She watches the homeless and spots a homeless family. She gets closer and speaks to the woman of the family, whose name is Chloe.

ALBERTINA: Hello! Do you live here? Do you always sleep here?

CHLOE: Yes, my family and I have no other home.

ALBERTINA: I don't have anywhere to spend the night with my son. Can I stay here with you?

CHLOE: Sure, dear, this is the first time for us! We feel out of place. You can stay here by my side. There is enough space for you. Where is your kid?

ALBERTINA: I am going to fetch him and get my stuff. I'll be right back. What's your name?

CHLOE: Chloe! Yours?

ALBERTINA: Albertina! I'll be right back.

Albertina walks quickly to the house.

At the same time, Lord Edwin and Patrick approach Constantino's house. Edwin pounds on the door. When Constantino opens it, Edwin and Patrick push their way inside, and Patrick closes the door. Edwin punches Constantino.

EDWIN: You bastard liar! Tell me her name and where she lives.

Edwin continues to punch Constantino until he falls to the floor. Edwin takes a chair and sits in front of Constantino.

CONSTANTINO: *(trying to catch his breath)* Give me a moment—

EDWIN: I have all the time in the world … *(laughs ironically)* right, Patrick? We can stay here all night long.

PATRICK: That's right … but if you want, I can solve this right now, my lord.

Constantino has a headache and speaks in a weak voice.

CONSTANTINO: Leave me alone … I know nothing.

EDWIN: Yes, you do … you know too much! You just don't want to talk. You are crap, Constantino! I can't understand how you could be a painter, someone who portrays the feminine soul so precisely, with so much delicacy. Something does not make sense …

PATRICK: Perhaps he wants to be one of them …

Constantino gets up and sits on the sofa, nursing a headache. He has been beaten so badly that he ought to have been unconscious for some minutes, but he is too selfish and nasty for that.

Meanwhile, Albertina is back at Adele's house.

ADELE: How was it? Did he pay you?

ALBERTINA: No … it was worse than I thought. He attacked me.

ADELE: I am sorry! You didn't deserve that … I never imagined he would do that.

ALBERTINA: Neither did I. I am really disappointed, Mrs Adele … my world fell apart! I feel like a tramp, with no value.

ADELE: On the contrary, you are very treasured, my dear. You are honest—you were only trying to make some money.

Albertina looks at William sleeping on the floor.

ALBERTINA: I have to wake William. Let me pick up my stuff. They should be on their way to take the keys. You must go.

ADELE: And you? I am worried, I wanted to help you …

Albertina hugs Adele.

ALBERTINA: You have helped me a lot, Mrs. Adele. I want to thank you for all that you have done for me and my son. I shall never forget you …

Albertina and Adele hold hands and smile.

ALBERTINA: I'll sleep at the home of an acquaintance from the market. I have just bumped into her, don't worry.

ADELE: *(smiles widely)* Thank the Lord! I am fine now.

ALBERTINA: So am I … good. I will wake William. Son? Son?

William awakes slowly.

ALBERTINA: We must go, William.

Albertina puts their clothes in a bag. Adele is ready to leave the house but waits for Albertina. They leave together. Adele and Albertina say goodbye on the sidewalk.

ADELE: I didn't mean for it to be like this, my dear. I really am sorry. If it wasn't for the situation of my sick sister, I could give you more attention, help you more. I like you as a daughter, Albertina. Your story moves me a lot; I know how hard it is to lose your husband and be alone like you. May God protect you, my dear. You know where to find me. If you need anything, count on me.

Albertina hugs Adele.

ALBERTINA: Thank you for everything you've done for me. You have an amazing heart. I hope to see you soon.

They smile. Adele touches Albertina's hair and kisses William goodbye. They part. Albertina walks towards the train station.

ALBERTINA: Look, William … right there, a new friend for you.

CHLOE: Hello! Stay here beside me, put your bag here!

ALBERTINA: Thank you, Chloe! This is William.

Nights start they make a bed for Albertina and William on the ground.

Meanwhile, Edwin and Patrick are still at the house of Constantino, whom they are brutally interrogating.

EDWIN: I won't go anywhere until you tell me her name and where she lives.

Edwin takes out his belt and beats Constantino. Constantino is on the floor powerless. Edwin grabs his hair.

EDWIN: If you don't talk, I'll beat you more …

CONSTANTINO: Albertina … her name is Albertina. She lives on the first corner after the train station. Green door with a hanging pot of flowers.

Edwin lets his head down and looks to Patrick.

PATRICK: Come quickly! Let him be.

Edwin sees the portrait of Albertina portrait wrapped in a bedsheet and gestures for Patrick to grab it.

Edwin and Patrick walk quickly towards Albertina's house, but when they get there, there's a "for sale" sign outside.

EDWIN: How is that possible, Patrick? He lied again!

PATRICK: No, wait! It is here—the green door with a flower. The corner after the train station. Let's ask around.

EDWIN: Excuse-me? Do you know who lives here?

PASSER-BY: No, I'm not from here.

EDWIN: Let's keep asking.

Edwin and Patrick cross the street and ask some people, but no one knows. They look at the house and see a man at the door, about to enter.

EDWIN: Hey, you! Wait!

The gentleman turns to look at them.

EDWIN: I want to know about the girl who lives at this house.

GENTLEMAN: I don't really know her. They left the house today. I've put it up for sale and have just come to check that it is empty.

PATRICK: We are looking for an estate to buy. Might we see it?

GENTLEMAN: Yes, of course. Come in.

They go inside the house, and Patrick keeps the seller busy with conversation while Edwin searches for any sign of Albertina. Edwin spots a small bottle of sandalwood oil left behind the bedside table and puts it in his pocket.

EDWIN: Patrick, this is not possible. I can't believe it. Did she really live here, and did she leave just today? Or is that pathetic lying again? An empty house without any sign of her!

PATRICK: I'm also confused … Please, sir, we are looking for the woman who lived here. Do you know anything?

GENTLEMAN: I only know that they had left in a hurry because of a sick sister, and I don't know where they went.

Patrick tries to learn more about the former resident but the seller knows nothing further. They thank the man and leave.

Edwin and Patrick start walking back to where they had left the carriage near Constantino's house. At the corner next to the train station, they stop to look before crossing. When Edwin looks to his left, he sees the people camped on the sidewalk. A profile captures his attention, a woman dressing a child. At this distance, Edwin can not be sure, but he stares at Albertina and thinks it's the woman they're looking for.

EDWIN: It's her, looks a lot like her.

PATRICK: Do you really think she would be here *(laughs)* sleeping on the street? Let's go, you are tired.

EDWIN: You're right … let's go!

And it was Albertina, Edwin's instinct was right. They walk back to the carriage. Although it would be wonderful for Lord Edwin to find the woman in the painting at this moment, they cannot even imagine she would be there. And Albertina, poor thing, is shyly adjusting herself among the homeless people.

Edwin and Patrick go back to the earl's house, and the night goes by. With dawn comes a twist of fate for Albertina.

CHAPTER 7

RE-ENCOUNTER

Anne walks through the street and approaches the train station crossing. At the same time, Albertina is leading William by the hand as they wander the streets. As both women approach the corner, the wind kicks up and sends the papers Anne carries flying. As she tries to chase them down, a paper comes to rest by Albertina's feet, and they both bend down to pick it up. When Anne looks up, Albertina smiles, and she recognizes her rescuer right away.

ANNE: Albertina! I am so glad I ran into you. I think about you so often. How have you been? I need to tell you so many things that happened after that day.

ALBERTINA: Oh, hello! I am fine. And you? It's good to see you … I apologize, but I don't recall your name.

ANNE: Anne! Remember you helped me?

ALBERTINA: Anne! Of course I do. I hope you have recovered.

ANNE: I have. What are you doing now? Is this your son?

Anne pats William on the head.

ALBERTINA: Yes! William, say hello to Anne … So, Anne, I am in a very delicate moment. I used to live with a lady who helped me, but yesterday she had to go and give the house back. I had to sleep on the sidewalk—

Anne looks shocked, feeling pity, and cuts her off.

ANNE: No! We can't have that. Not after you were so kind to me. Grab your stuff right away and come with me. We'll go to the shop.

ALBERTINA: What shop?

ANNE: The one you took me to when you rescued me. You have no idea what a good thing you did! I am working there and am engaged to the owner, Phil!

ALBERTINA: I don't believe it! *(laughs)* It must be fate! but should I go there with you?

ANNE: For both of us. We'll help you, don't worry. Now, where are your things?

ALBERTINA: Over here …

They fetch her bags, and Albertina says goodbye to Chloe.

ANNE: Let's go this way.

They talk as they walk along.

ANNE: On that day, we didn't have a chance to get to know each other. Where did you live? What about your family?

ALBERTINA: My husband died some time ago, and since then I have been helped by some people. The lady I used to live with needed to go all of a sudden.

ANNE: I am so glad I met you! I am very happy, Albertina.

ALBERTINA: Thank you, Anne. I don't know how to thank you for this.

ANNE: You don't have to. I want to thank you for all you did for me.

They arrive at the shop. They enter, and Phil is there.

Anne: Look who I brought with me! I bumped into Albertina on the street.

Albertina greets Phil.

Anne: And this is William, her son.

Phil: Wonderful, Albertina! Anne thinks of you often, and so do I. You brought us together, without knowing it.

Albertina: She told me. *(laughs)* I am very glad to know!

Anne: Well, Phil, Albertina has no place to live right now, so I invited her to stay here for a while. There's the room behind the shop …

Phil: *(with a big smile)* Of course! It will be a great pleasure to have you here. After you get settled in, I might have an offer for you.

Anne: *(laughs)* I think I know what it is …

Albertina: An offer? I am curious …

Anne: Come, Albertina, first I'll show you your room. This way.

Anne opens the door, and Albertina enters. It's a big room with a red velvet, comfortable-looking double bed, beige curtains, an beige umbrella-shaped lamp with golden fringe, a noble wood dressing table with a mirror, and a wood floor. Albertina is amazed, covering her mouth with her hand.

Albertina: Oh my, it's beautiful! What a beautiful bed! I am surprised and so very grateful, Anne!

Anne: I am really happy to have you here! I am very glad you like it.

William gets in the bed.

ALBERTINA: Have some rest, son. You are tired, right? Once again, thanks for having me here at your house, Anne.

ANNE: My pleasure. I have to tell you, after that day, Phil walked me home, and we talked on the way. By the time we got to my house, he had offered me a job at the shop, and I said yes.

ALBERTINA: It's a beautiful story. I am glad to know that.

ANNE: As the time passed by, we got closer … so he proposed. *(laughs)*

ALBERTINA: He looks in love indeed, and you are a beautiful couple.

Phil slips into the room.

PHIL: Good fortune brings you here, Albertina. I was wondering if you would like to work here at the shop.

ALBERTINA: A job? I don't believe it! Of course I would, it's a dream job.

PHIL: I lost my last employee when I proposed her. I want Anne to take more care of store administration, purchases and payments.

The three of them laugh.

ANNE: But she'll start tomorrow! Today we'll talk about everything. I want Albertina to come with me to my house so I can try on my wedding dress. I scheduled the seamstress for this evening.

ALBERTINA: I love to see brides. Getting married is very exciting!

That afternoon, Anne and Albertina walk through the streets to Anne's house.

ANNE: Albertina, I'm embarrassed to tell you, but my mother is a bitter person. I don't want you to be alarmed if she picks on me, or speaks against the marriage and so on. She's always in a bad mood. She never agrees with anything.

ALBERTINA: Oh, my God, I'm so sorry. Don't worry. It's a special moment, so let's focus on the dress. I am eager to see you as a bride! Love is so beautiful. *(laughs)*

They arrive at the house and go in.

ANNE: Mother? Mother!

MARGOT: I'm here!

ANNE: This is Albertina, the girl who rescued me. Remember?

MARGOT: I do remember! Hello, dear. How are you?

ANNE: Has the seamstress come?

MARGOT: Nobody has come here. Are you making a dress?

ANNE: Yes, Mother, a wedding dress.

MARGOT: A wedding dress?

ANNE: I've told you Phil has proposed to me.

MARGOT: I didn't know it would be so fast.

Margot seems not to enjoy the news. There is a knock on the door. It's the seamstress. Ana takes her to the bedroom, and Albertina goes with them.

ALBERTINA: It's beautiful!

ANNE: Let me see it … I'll try it on!

ALBERTINA: Anne, it's perfect! You look dazzling.

Margot stands in the hall, overhearing with envy towards her daughter.

ANNE: It's really beautiful, the way I wanted it … There are only few alternations to be made. Albertina? Can you bring me the pearl necklace in that box, please? Let's see how it looks.

ALBERTINA: Beautiful … what a gorgeous bride!

Margot can't hold back her curiosity and enters the bedroom. She glares at her daughter.

MARGOT: It's a pity it won't last!

Albertina stares at Anne's mother, uncomfortable.

ANNE: We can't know how long it will last!

MARGOT: True! But sooner or later, he'll dump you.

ANNE: I am not interested on your negative words. What matters is this moment I am living.

The seamstress continues fitting the dress on Anne's body.

MARGOT: Sure, enjoy it. But be sure it will over before you know it.

Albertina is impressed by Anne's mother's bad mood and changes the subject.

ALBERTINA: Don't you think this is a beautiful dress?

MARGOT: Every wedding dress is beautiful, even the ugliest of them.

ANNE: *(to the seamstress)* You may go now. Tomorrow I'll bring the dress back to you. Thank you.

The seamstress leaves. Anne keeps looking at herself in the mirror and smiling.

ANNE: I am so happy … it's a beautiful dress.

MARGOT: You won't stay happy! It's an illusion.

ANNE: Enough! Stop being bitter! You are disgraceful.

Albertina tries to get between them, but Margot's expression is full of hate as she lunges at Anne. She rips the dress and pulls on the necklace until it breaks. Anne clutches the pearls to her throat.

MARGOT: He'll dump you! You won't be happy!

Anne and Albertina run desperately out of the house and into the street. Anne, still wearing her wedding dress and trying to hold the string of pearls together, cries nonstop and leans in a tree. Albertina, deeply moved by the situation, hugs Anne.

Albertina ponders life and realises that Anne also has problems and difficulties. But she is a strong young woman, she thinks, who does not allow herself to be shattered by the out-of-control mother she has. And I, who thought I was unfortunate for having lost my husband and having lost my parents so early … but that's life. It goes on.

Anne keeps crying and trying to hold together her pearls. They walk towards Phil's store.

At the store, Phil is at the counter assisting Edwin, who has his back to the door as Anne and Albertina arrive from across the counter, Phil sees Anne crying, Edwin at first does not turn, and when Anne drops a few pearls, Edwin look, but at the same time Albertina kneels to catch them behind the counter and they go into Albertina's room and close the door. Edwin has no idea that Albertina is so close.

PHIL: Lord Edwin! Excuse me, please, I'll be right back.

Phil knocks on the door to Albertina's room, and she opens it.

ALBERTINA: I am so sorry, Mr Phil!

Anne is still sobbing, sitting on the bed. Phil sits by her side, lays her head on his chest, and speaks to Albertina.

PHIL: What happened? Margot?

ALBERTINA: Yes … she is a madwoman! She said Anne would never be happy, that you would leave her sooner or later. Anne asked her to be quiet, and then she attacked her and ripped her dress.

PHIL: *(angrily)* I'll settle this once and for all … Albertina, would you do me a favour? There's a client at the counter, Lord Edwin. Could you tell him that as soon as I get his goods, we'll take the samples to his house?

ALBERTINA: Certainly!

Albertina starts to leave the room to serve Lord Edwin, but Anne grasps her skirt to stop her.

ANNE: No! Leave her here, Phil. You go assist him and close the shop.

PHIL: All right, darling!

Phil kisses her on the forehead and goes to serves his customer and friend, Lord Edwin, says goodbye and leaves. Hours later, Phil closes the store.

Very upset that Anne was assaulted by her mother, he proposes that Anne come to live with him immediately and suggests that he go to her house with her to get her belongings. Still shaken and crying, Anne agree, but feels uncomfortable and is afraid of her mother being aggressive again. They walk arm-in-arm to Anne's house.

Margot is in the living room. She watches the two of them go upstairs to Anne's bedroom and follows them.

MARGOT: If you take your things from here, you can't ever come back!

ANNE: I don't want to!

MARGOT: You will when he dumps you.

PHIL: I'll never leave Anne because she is not like you, bitter and envious.

Phil faces down Margot angrily, and she leaves the room. Anne packs her things and goes downstairs with Phil.

ANNE: You always knew you would end up alone, but I've never thought you would be completely alone., without your daughter, friends. or husband …

MARGOT: You'll end up like this too.

Anne: No, I won't!

Phil takes Anne in his arms and kisses her in front of Margot. Then they look at her and go back to the shop. The door closes, and the world of Margot falls down.

In tears, this bitter and solitary mother loses her daughter to happiness. Margot will have to live in silence, without anyone to insult or to share her poison, her sadness, and her negative perspective that the world is unjust and without love. This silence will always be a reminder of how happy Anne is with her husband.

I's night when Phil and Anne return to the shop, Albertina is there to greet them.

Albertina: Are you all right? Let me help you …

Anne: We are all right! But she was bitter as always.

Phil: Have the orders arrived?

Albertina: Yes, I placed them here because I don't where they belong.

Phil: It's fine, I'll show you tomorrow.

Anne and Phil take her belongings upstairs. Albertina and Willian go to sleep. The next day Phil shows Albertina how to organize the goods.

Phil: Let's open this box … oh, Lord Edwin's new fabric. Look, Albertina. I'll cut the samples, and you can take them to the customer in the afternoon.

Albertina: Yes, of course!

They keep working in the shop and tidying up. Phil is at the till checking invoices and making calculations, Anne takes care of the window and display of new products. Albertina dusts the shelves and organizes all the products. In the afternoon Phil cuts the Sample fabrics.

Phil: Let's separate this one. That other is also pretty …

ALBERTINA: I like this green … look at this navy bue!

PHIL: Yes, cut them!

Phil finishes separating the sample fabrics.

PHIL: Here they are, Albertina!

Before Albertina leaves the shop, she smooths sandalwood oil on her hands. Then she takes the fabric samples and gets into the carriage to go to Edwin's house.

CHAPTER

8

THE BIG DATE

At Lord Edwin's house, Oswald is encouraging another of his dinner parties. After all Oswald loves parties and social gatherings, Edwin is quieter and after the death of his wife Helena he became discouraged and makes an effort to participate in social gatherings. Besides, Edwin is not pleased with any woman who has crossed his path.

OSWALD: I am sure a dinner will cheer you up, my friend! You need to get back to your old self, the one before you started buying these paintings. *(laughs)*

EDWIN: Perhaps you are right. *(laughs)* Patrick said I am crazy already.

They hear a carriage brought up for Oswald.

OSWALD: Well, I must go now. I'll see you in four days for the our dinner!

EDWIN: I can't wait! *(laughs)*

OSWALD: You bastard! *(laughs)* You will thank me one day!

Edwin walks Oswald out to his carriage.

EDWIN: I'll thank you if you find the girl on the painting for me and invite her to our dinner. *(laughs)*

The carriages leaves, and Edwin waves to his friend. He goes back inside and searches for Patrick.

EDWIN: Patrick? Patrick!

PATRICK: Yes, Lord Edwin!

EDWIN: Come to town with me, quickly! I want to search for Albertina before night falls.

PATRICK: Yes! The carriage is ready, we may go.

They get in the coach and head for town, Edwin thinking about Albertina. On the way, the carriage with Albertina is also coming, they pass each other. Once again they don't see each other.

Albertina gets out of the carriage and sees Edwin's mansion. Impressed, she walks slowly, gazing at the beautiful gardens and entrance of the house. Thinking that she has never seen anything like this before, she walks up the steps to the main entrance and stops in front of the huge and imposing front door. She looks from side to side for someone to help her, but she sees no one. She knocks on the door and waits … she knocks one more time, but nobody answers. She goes down the steps and around the house.

ALBERTINA: Hello? Anybody home?

Albertina keeps walking through the yard and calling out until she finds a door. The house's cook, Judith, opens a small window beside the door.

ALBERTINA: Hello, I've brought this to Lord Edwin on behalf of Mr Phil.

JUDITH: It's all right, miss. I'll handle it.

ALBERTINA: Thank you. Goodbye.

Judith receives the package and take it up to place on the bedside table in Edwin's bedroom as Albertina goes back to the carriage.

The afternoon falls Lord Edwin and Patrick are riding around town in the carriage trying to find Albertina.

EDWIN: I won't give up, Patrick. I feel I will meet her.

PATRICK: Yes, I understand, but we are tired. We have to get back! It's late.

EDWIN: You're right, let's go.

Edwin returns home and after dinner goes to sleep. At morning he wakes up to the smell of sandalwood surrounding him. He looks around to see where it is coming from and sees the bundle of fabrics at the bedside. He picks it up to smell, and it's the source of the sandalwood. He jumps out of his bed, opens a drawer, and brings out the bottle of sandalwood he found at Albertina's house.

EDWIN: It smells the same! Or am I mad?

Edwin sniffs back and forth to compare the scents of the bottle and the bundle for a while, then leaves them on the bed and to sniff at the paintings from which he had first smelled the sandalwood scent.

EDWIN: It's weaker, but I think it is the same! Can it hers, the scent on the fabric samples?

Edwin runs through the house looking for Maria, his housekeeper.

EDWIN: Maria? Maria!

MARIA: Yes, Lord Edwin?

EDWIN: Who brought these fabrics here?

MARIA: I don't know. I wasn't here. Judith the cook received them. They came from Mr Phil's shop.

EDWIN: I need to talk to Judith …

Edwin goes to the kitchen.

EDWIN: Judith! Who brought this package here?

JUDITH: It was a beautiful young lady, My Lord, but I only received it and she left.

EDWIN: What did she look like?

JUDITH: Fair skin, long chestnut hair, bright eyes …

EDWIN: Wait! I'll be right back.

Edwin goes to his bedroom, gets one of the paintings of Albertina, and brings it to show Judith.

EDWIN: Did she look like the woman in this painting?

JUDITH: Yes, that's her! Or somebody who looks very much like her.

Edwin smiles with the knowledge that he is closer to finding Albertina.

EDWIN: Thank you, Judith!

Edwin goes back to his room and gets dressed quickly. He's so anxious that he barely eats his breakfast. Patrick brings round the carriage.

PATRICK: My Lord? It's all set. Whenever you want.

EDWIN: We must go now!

The carriage goes the same path as always, but this time, Edwin looks at the beautiful trees with a heart full of hope and peace. He puts his head out the window and fills his lungs with the cool breeze, looking at the blue sky and the rays of sunshine that pass through the trees and come to touch his face. He smiles, feeling like a lucky guy. His desire to find Albertina is so great that his senses have been sharpened, the smell of sandalwood wouldn't leave this infatuated man's mind. They have been close to each other the whole time!

EDWIN: Patrick, stop the carriage. I'll walk from here.

PATRICK: Yes, My Lord! I'll wait for you here.

Edwin walks in a hurry towards Phil's shop and arrives breathless. Albertina is behind the counter with her back turned to the entrance. Edwin leans on the counter, barely able to breathe. Albertina turns and looks at him.

ALBERTINA: Hello! How may I assist you?

Edwin is speechless, tired and dizzy after his run. Albertina puts her hand over his.

ALBERTINA: Are you all right? Would you like a drink of water?

EDWIN: Yes! I need water.

Albertina turns and goes in the back to fetch water. Lord Edwin watches his sweet passion in disbelief that he has found her.

ALBERTINA: Here it is! Please, have a seat.

Albertina pulls out a chair for Edwin and remains standing by his side. Edwin recovers little by little and can't take eyes off Albertina. She starts to feel embarrassed by the intensity of his gaze. William comes into the shop.

WILLIAM: What happened to him, Mom?

ALBERTINA: Nothing, William … go back to your room!

EDWIN: William? What a beautiful name. How old are you?

WILLIAM: Almolst four!

Edwin gets up and picks William up in his arms.

EDWIN: What type of games do you like to play?

WILLIAM: Shooting, riding carriages …

EDWIN: Carriages! Would you like to go for a ride with me?

Edwin puts William on the floor and walks towards Albertina to greet her, kissing her hand.

EDWIN: Nice to meet you, Miss! I'm Edwin.

ALBERTINA: Albertina. I went to your house yesterday.

Edwin whispers into her ear.

EDWIN: I know, I woke up with your smell!

Albertina does not understand.

EDWIN: Where's Phil?

ALBERTINA: I'll call him!

Albertina goes into the back and returns with Phil, who is smiling.

PHIL: It's nice to have you here! How are you?

EDWIN: I am fine, thank you. I got your fabric samples. Could I borrow your employee to help me match the fabric and measure?

PHIL: Of course! Could you go with him, Albertina?

ALBERTINA: Yes, Mr Phil.

EDWIN: William, do you want to go for a carriage ride?

William nods. Edwin takes him in his arms again and says goodbye to Phil. Albertina and Edwin walk to the carriage.

EDWIN: Patrick! We're back. This is Albertina and William.

PATRICK: Hello!

Albertina smiles, and they get in the carriage and set off. After some minutes.

EDWIN: I am sorry for asking, but are you married?

ALBERTINA: No …

WILLIAM: She is a sad widow.

Albertina and Edwin laugh at William.

EDWIN: I am sorry. Would you like to marry again? Albertina.

ALBERTINA: *(sighs)* It's not that simple …

EDWIN: You are pretty, you must be courted all the time.

ALBERTINA: *(laughs)* No, I'm not. In fact my husband passed away not so long ago, and my life got really difficult. I am very busy just trying to survive and take care of my son.

EDWIN: I see … you haven't answered, though. Would you like to remarry and have a family?

ALBERTINA: Perhaps … yes.

EDWIN: Where do you live?

ALBERTINA: I'm living at Mr Phil's house.

EDWIN: Oh, so you are in good hands!

ALBERTINA: They are very nice, indeed. Ana is a dear.

At Edwin's house, Edwin and Albertina go into the main hall. Edwin is showing her how he wants to change the décor.

EDWIN: I want to cover the whole wall … I need something to match these curtains.

ALBERTINA: Yes, Lord Edwin! What do you think of this one? Or that one? I think they both match.

They talk and gesture, and Edwin sometimes puts his hands on her shoulder as Albertina takes notes.

EDWIN: Let's have some tea?

ALBERTINA: Yes, thank you!

After they take tea, Edwin shows her the garden, Willian is happily running around the garden.

ALBERTINA: Oh my, it's beautiful!

As they walk, Edwin plucks a rose and gives to Albertina.

EDWIN: For you, lovely lady.

She begins to feel happy and starts to feel better by his side.

ALBERTINA: Thank you, it's the most beautiful rose I've ever received.

Edwin stou are the most beautiful lady I ever gave a rose.

ALBERTINA: *(laughs)* Thank you!

EDWIN: Albertina, would you like to have dinner with me tomorrow?

ALBERTINA: Yes, of course! Thank you for the invitation.

That evening, Albertina and Anne are sitting on the bed talking about the day she's had.

ALBERTINA: Then he gave me this rose *(laughs)*.

ANNE: I am very glad for you, Albertina! I think he is fond of you.

ALBERTINA: He invited me to dinner tomorrow.

ANNE: Well, we need to find you a dress! Mine will be too loose and won't fit you. But first thing tomorrow, I can go to Margaret di M*édici*'s house and ask to borrow something. She is my friend, don't worry.

ALBERTINA: Oh my, thank you, Anne!

Anne has been received at the Duchess's house the next day. Margaret was Phil's most important customer. And he always talked a lot with Anne.

MARGARET: Have a seat, darling!

ANNE: Thank you, Your Grace. I was wondering—I need a dress in Isabel's size. Do you have one she doesn't use anymore, or something older? It's for a friend.

MARGARET: Of course, Anne! It's not a problem at all. I had a new one made for her, but she didn't like it. *(laughs)*

Margaret has a maid bring the dress.

ANNE: Ah. It looks perfect to me.

MARGARET: I thought so.

ANNE: It really turned out beautifully … I remember when I sold you the fabric!

MARGARET: Yes, you said it would be beautiful, but Isabel doesn't like delicate dresses.

ANNE: I am speechless! You are very kind!

They talk for a while, and then Anne goes back to the store. Anne enters the shop with the dress and goes to Albertina's room.

ANNE: Albertina! Come and see …

Anne gets the dress from the bag and puts it on Albertina's bed.

ALBERTINA: My God! It's gorgeous …

ANNE: Yes, and I think it's going to fit you perfectly!

Later, as Albertina is nearly finished getting dressed, Anne knocks on her door.

ANNE: Albertina? Patrick is waiting outside.

Albertina opens the door.

ALBERTINA: I am ready!

Anne is dazzled.

ANNE: Albertina, you are gorgeous!

They both laugh in joy. Then Albertina looks into Anne's eyes.

ALBERTINA: But I'm really worried … I don't feel comfortable, even though I know I look beautiful in this dress. Life has stolen my hopes. It seems like I don't deserve this dinner, or it's all a lie … I don't know, I feel a grip on my heart.

ANNE: Don't think about it, Albertina. You do deserve the love of a man like Lord Edwin. You're a beautiful and kind lady. I understand that life has hurt you. I also lost my value with the disappointments of life, but we need to turn it around. If he likes you, no one or anything that happens will change that. Love always speaks louder, and we need to believe in love.

ALBERTINA: Thank you! I must leave now.

CHAPTER 9

SWEET PASSION

Patrick is in the carriage outside waiting for Albertina when she appears, beautiful and shy. He helps her into the carriage. Albertina becomes lost on her thoughts, but Patrick strikes up a conversation.

> PATRICK: Lord Edwin is looking forward to your dinner, Albertina.
>
> ALBERTINA: Really? How do you know that?
>
> PATRICK: Well, he told me.
>
> ALBERTINA: Oh! *(laughs)* What else did he tell you?
>
> PATRICK: A few things. *(laughs)* But it's a secret …

Albertina laughs.

At Edwin's house, the carriages of the guests are arriving. Edwin and Oswald is receiving the guests at the main door.

Margaret di *Médici* arrives with Isabel, and they greet Edwin. Moments later Albertina arrives approaches Edwin, smiling. Isabel sees Albertina in her dress and is consumed with anger.

> ISABEL: What's this? I can't believe … Albertina!

MARGARET: Shut up!

ISABEL: No, I won't!

Isabel storms towards Albertina. Edwin notices that something is wrong and looks at both of them. Margaret grasps Isabel's shoulder.

ISABEL: Take off my dress right away!

Albertina does not understand and stares at her.

MARGARET: Isabel! I am not kidding, that's enough.

Isabel shakes her off and waves her arms.

ISABEL: Oh, you will take it off, darling. This is my dress, and I haven't even worn it yet. Take it off now.

ALBERTINA: This your dress? I am sorry, My Lady, I didn't know … Anne lent it to me.

Edwin stares at them. He is sick of Isabel, and everyone is staring.

MARGARET: No, my darling, I lent it! It is *my* dress.

Oswald is staring at them.

ISABEL: No, it's mine! Either you take it off, or I will.

MARGARET: I'll teach you a lesson when we get home …

EDWIN: Let me fix this, ladies …

ISABEL: Thank you, My Lord, it's very kind of you.

Edwin whispers to Oswald. He waves Patrick over.

EDWIN: Miss Albertina, come with me, please. You too, Patrick. I've told Oswald to greet the guests. Tell him also to seat the guests at their places. I'll have the dinner served soon enough. I won't take part in it …

PATRICK: What will I say?

EDWIN: Tell them I'll be right there, but I am feeling unwell.

PATRICK: All right, My Lord.

EDWIN: After the dinner starts, come to the hall to take Isabel's dress. I'll ask Maria to fetch one of the cook's dresses.

PATRICK: I'm on my way!

Edwin takes Albertina's hand and leads her through the hall to the kitchen.

ALBERTINA: My Lord? I apologize for all this embarrassment!

EDWIN: Don't say that!

Edwin places his hand on her face, slides his fingers onto her lips.

EDWIN: I am the one to ask your forgiveness, Albertina … you are not to blame. I did not tell you I would have more guests.

ALBERTINA: Thank you, I am feeling a bit better.

Albertina gazes into Edwin's eyes, and their faces draw close. Edwin stares at Albertina's lips. Maria enters the hall and startles them.

MARIA: I'm sorry, My Lord, I didn't know you were here.

EDWIN: Maria, I need you! This is Albertina. I need a uniform dress, so Albertina can change.

MARIA: Yes, sir. Albertina, come with me.

Maria takes Albertina to the maids' room.

MARIA: I'll take one from Judith. You have the same size. Now get dressed!

Albertina gets dressed, and it fits perfectly.

ALBERTINA: It's great. Thank you, Maria.

Edwin is waiting in the hall, now wearing a cook's uniform. Albertina sees him and laughs

EDWIN: You look pretty …

ALBERTINA: Thank you, *Mr* Edwin … and you've changed your clothes!

EDWIN: You don't need to call me mister. Call me Edwin! Do you like my outfit?

They laugh. Edwin decides not to return to the dining room so as not to further humiliate Albertina. And also to teach Isabel a lesson, who is an arrogant, selfish person and humiliates people without mercy. On the left side of the dining room there is a door that gives access to a small hall with a small floral sofa and a corridor that connects the small hall to the kitchen.

EDWIN: Let's sit here. Come.

They sit behind the main hall door on a floral sofa and wait for the food to be served. When the staff go back to the kitchen, Edwin takes Albertina's hand.

EDWIN: I am really sorry for what happened to you, but I am glad to be here by your side, just the two of us.

ALBERTINA: Why do you say these things to me? You're confusing me. I don't know what to believe.

EDWIN: I understand … I must seem utterly mad! We met only yesterday, and yet I am behaving as if we have met before, am I not?

ALBERTINA: Yes, that's it. You are very kind to me, as if I was somebody very close to you.

EDWIN: Tonight, we'll dine together, just you and I. No one will stand between us, and you will understand many things.

Patrick goes in to get Isabel's dress, enters the dining room where the guests are seated. He gently tosses it over the back of her chair.

PATRICK: Here it is, My Lady.

ISABEL: Thank you!

Margaret shakes her head, disapproving of Isabel's attitude.

ISABEL: Patrick? Where's Lord Edwin?

PATRICK: He will be here soon! He is feeling unwell. He has asked the guests to keep enjoying the dinner and to make themselves comfortable.

OSWALD: Great! We will have fun. And tell him we will eat all the food!

They all laugh.

ISABEL: I am sure he regrets inviting that *maid* who embarrassed him, and doesn't want to come back. He might have said goodbye to her at the back door.

Isabel seems satisfied with this resolution.

MARGARET: Let's go home, Isabel. Everyone is leaving, and I am tired.

They get up and say goodbye to Oswald.

Maria starts clearing the table with the other servants and set up again. Edwin returns to have his dinner with Albertina.

EDWIN: I finally get to eat—I am starving. *(laughs)*

ALBERTINA: *(laughs with him)* So am I.

EDWIN: A glass of wine for my lovely guest?

ALBERTINA: Yes, thank you! My Lord, do you live here by yourself?

EDWIN: Yes, my darling, that's why I am so happy with you here.

ALBERTINA: How could a man like you not have anybody? You are handsome and rich! A charming man …

EDWIN: It's nice of you to have thoughts like these about me. *(laughs)* I was married once, but my wife died a while ago, and we had no children.

ALBERTINA: I am sorry!

EDWIN: Yes, but things have changed. I am in love again!

ALBERTINA: *(clueless)* That's good!

Edwin stares at Albertina, wishing to laugh.

EDWIN: Now that we have finished dinner, I'll show you who is occupying my heart. I need all your attention to tell you a beautiful story.

Edwin takes Albertina's hand.

ALBERTINA: I love to hear stories …

EDWIN: Some time ago, I met a wonderful woman. I fell in love with her at first sight. However, I didn't know anything about her, not even her name! Since then I've searched for her.

ALBERTINA: Oh my! It's a beautiful story. You are so romantic. But did you ever find her?

Edwin gets up from the table and leads Albertina by the hand.

EDWIN: I'll show you.

He takes her through the hall to his bedroom.

EDWIN: Wait! Close your eyes.

He places his hands over her eyes. Edwin and Albertina slowly enter his room. When they are in front of the paintings, he gently removes his hands from Albertina's eyes. Albertina is shocked, covering her mouth with her hands. She gets closer to the paintings and bursts in tears. He guides her to sit next to him on the edge of his bed and places his arms around her shoulders.

ALBERTINA: So, it was you who bought all the paintings?

EDWIN: Yes, I bought all of them, and I have been searching for you ever since. Let me show you something else.

Edwin opens the drawer in the nightstand and brings out the empty bottle of sandalwood.

ALBERTINA: Is that mine? Where did you get it?

EDWIN: At the house where you used to live.

ALBERTINA: You've been there?

EDWIN: Do you remember at Phil's shop when you told me you had been at my house? I replied, "I know, I woke up with your scent."

ALBERTINA: Yes, and I didn't understand.

EDWIN: Your sandalwood was left on the samples you brought me.

Albertina looks into Edwin's eyes.

EDWIN: Albertina, now I have found you, I want you to stay with me for the rest of our lives.

Edwin puts his hand on Albertina's face and kisses her madly.

EDWIN: Albertina! I love you!

They kiss more and more. After some moments, they go back to the dining hall, where the table has been cleared. Edwin asks for more wine and then orders the servants not to enter.

EDWIN: More wine for my beloved lady …

Edwin serves Albertina. After a few sips, he has her stand. He opens her dress and leaves her naked. He pulls her onto the dining table and gently kisses her. Slowly he opens his trousers, and they make love. Edwin slides his hand over her beautiful body.

After a long night, they wake up in bed. Edwin asked the servants for breakfast in bed.

They have breakfast together. Then Edwin takes Albertina's hands.

EDWIN: Albertina, will you marry me?

Albertina looks at him amazed and in love.

ALBERTINA: Of course I will!

EDWIN: Tomorrow I'll fetch your things and our son! You will live here.

ALBERTINA: Everything is so fast … you are a wonderful man.

EDWIN: I'll talk to Mr Phil when I take you back.

ALBERTINA: Lord Edwin, it was the best night of my life. I loved every moment by your side. I'm still not buying all of this. Shall we go now? I need to see William.

Days pass. Albertina is in a beautiful dress of black lace, with beautiful jewellery. Edwin looks very elegant, as usual. William is playing with Maria, and Patrick has arranged the carriage.

ALBERTINA: Shall I know where are we going, my love?

EDWIN: No, darling—remember, it's a surprise!

They say goodbye to Maria and William and get into the carriage. Soon they arrive at the fair. Albertina has no idea this was where the paintings of her were sold. They get out and start to walk around. Edwin makes sure they will pass through the painters' stalls. Albertina stops near a china stall, but Edwin spots Constantino and approaches him.

CONSTANTINO: My Lord? how have you been? I have new paintings!

EDWIN: I am great …

Edwin looks at the paintings, but none of them have Albertina's beauty.

EDWIN: You may offer them to my lady, Constantino. She is right over there. If she wants them, I'll buy them all!

Albertina has her back to the stall, wearing a beautiful hat and with her hair done up. Constantino walks towards her, full of joy.

CONSTANTINO: My Lady!

Albertina turns, and Constantino, without looking into her face, kneels and kisses her hand. Then he looks up and realizes it's Albertina. She also recognizes him. He pretends he is not surprised to know about her and Edwin.

CONSTANTINO: My Lady, please come to see my works …

ALBERTINA: I am not interested!

CONSTANTINO: Please, My Lady, forget the past, I beg of you.

Albertina goes to look at Constantino's paintings, but none holds her attention.

ALBERTINA: I don't like any of them … but I can help you.

Albertina throws some coins at Constantino. She and Edwin walks away, embarrassed, Constantino watches the couple passing by the fair, elegant and full of prestige. Albertina is now a noble society lady.

Milton Keynes UK
Ingram Content Group UK Ltd.
UKHW050645201023
430935UK00008BA/52

9 781982 287498